Jon Scieszka's TRUCKTOWN
DIZZY IZZY

WRITTEN BY JON SCIESZKA

CHARACTERS AND ENVIRONMENTS DEVELOPED BY THE

DAVID SHANNON   LOREN LONG   DAVID GORDON

ILLUSTRATION CREW:

Executive producer: TOT INDUSTRIES in association with Animagic S.L.

Creative supervisor: Nina Rappaport Brown ○ Drawings by: Dan Root ○ Color by: Christopher Oatley

Art director: Karin Paprocki

READY-TO-ROLL

ALADDIN

NEW YORK   LONDON   TORONTO   SYDNEY

🏮 A L A D D I N

An imprint of Simon & Schuster Children's Publishing Division

1230 Avenue of the Americas, New York, NY 10020

First Aladdin paperback edition June 2010

Text and illustrations copyright © 2010 by JRS Worldwide, LLC.

for bulk purchases, please contact Simon & Schuster Special Sales at 1-866-506-1949
or business@simonandschuster.com.

The Simon & Schuster Speakers Bureau can bring authors to your live event. For more
information or to book an event contact the Simon & Schuster Speakers Bureau at
1-866-248-3049 or visit our website at www.simonspeakers.com. / The text of this book was set in Truck King.

Manufactured in United States of America / 0512 LAK / 10 9 8 7 6 5 4 3

Library of Congress Cataloging-in-Publication Data

Scieszka, Jon. / Dizzy Izzy / by Jon Scieszka ; artwork by the Design Garage: David Gordon.

Loren Long, David Shannon.—1st Aladdin ed. / p. cm.—(Trucktown. Ready-to-roll.)

Summary: Izzy the ice cream truck tries to get himself dizzy.

[1. Ice cream trucks—Fiction. 2. Trucks—Fiction.] I. Design Garage. II. Title. / PZ7.S41267Diz 2010

[E]—dc22 / 2008024360 / ISBN 978-1-4169-4145-3 (pbk) / ISBN 978-1-4169-4156-9 (hc)

This is Izzy.

Izzy loves to get dizzy.

But is he?

Izzy gets
busy.

Izzy skids in a tizzy.
But Izzy is not dizzy.

Is he?

Izzy gets fizzy.
But Izzy is not dizzy.

Is he?

THEN IZZY GETS AN IDEA.

"Do you want an ice cream?
Do you want an ice cream?
Do you want an ice cream?"

Izzy whizzes.

Izzy fizzes.

Izzy gets busy and fizzy
and all whizzy
in a tizzy.

But
guess
what?